# REFUGIA

**UNIVERSITY OF CALGARY**
Press

# REFUGIA

## Patrick Horner

Brave & Brilliant Series
ISSN 2371-7238 (Print) ISSN 2371-7246 (Online)

University of Calgary Press
2500 University Drive NW
Calgary, Alberta
Canada T2N 1N4
press.ucalgary.ca

LIBRARY AND ARCHIVES CANADA CATALOGUING IN PUBLICATION

Title: Refugia / Patrick Horner.
Names: Horner, Patrick, 1975- author.
Series: Brave & brilliant series ; no. 28.
Description: Series statement: Brave & brilliant series, 2371-7238 ; 28 | Poems.
Identifiers: Canadiana (print) 2022024202X | Canadiana (ebook) 20220242097 | ISBN
    9781773853727 (softcover) | ISBN 9781773853734 (PDF) | ISBN 9781773853741 (EPUB)
Classification: LCC PS8615.O7735 R44 2022 | DDC C811/.6—dc23

The University of Calgary Press acknowledges the support of the Government of Alberta
through the Alberta Media Fund for our publications. We acknowledge the financial support
of the Government of Canada. We acknowledge the financial support of the Canada Council
for the Arts for our publishing program.

Printed and bound in Canada by Marquis
♻ This book is printed on Opaque Smooth Natural paper

Cover image: Mary Delany, *Botanical Study*, ca. 1772-82, paper collage, 25.5 x 23.2 cm,
Harris Brisbane Dick Fund, 1925. Courtesy of the MET Collection API.

Editing by Helen Hajnoczky
Cover design, page design, and typesetting by Melina Cusano

*Throughout the history of modern biology, islands have featured in the study of evolution.*

J. Bristol Foster, "The evolution of the mammals of the Queen Charlotte Islands, British Columbia," *Occasional papers of the British Columbia Provincial Museum*, no. 14 (November 1965).

December 15, 1965

Dr. Moriarty
Department of Biology
Cunningham Building 202
University of Victoria
Victoria, B.C.

Dear Joe,

I am writing to convey the unfortunate news that Emily and Roland have still not been found. The local RCMP have called off the search. It has been 40 days since they were last seen, and the officials have reached the conclusion that they have either drowned or for whatever reason do not wish to be found. Their gear and supplies remain very much intact. If they left, they left with nothing.

I have enclosed a couple of notebooks and a collection of letters that were found in the research tent at their base camp. Due to the long hours involved in the search I have not been able to read through these. It is possible they offer some clue to their whereabouts but at this point I would consider it unlikely. It is possible their notes will provide insight into their findings and further their research on the refugia theory.

I am returning to the mainland tomorrow via the ferry. I know this news will weigh on you heavily. I am still holding onto a candle of hope. Take care and see you soon.

Sincerely,

James

1

april 5   electrophoresis

this is the beginning. when i arrived, emily was already waiting.
outside the blackbird cafe. the steady rain, an orderly disruption.
the darkness of night turned into day. an old man with a beard
stopped to tell me of an island to the south where the flowers have
no names. you've got your work cut out for you he said. emily
listened, making decisive notes in the margin of a used book. her
brown hair fell like rain over her brown eyes. she carried only a
small backpack and a leather satchel. the less of ourselves we bring
to the project the less we project onto it she said. john was supposed
to meet us at eight to take us to the boat, he arrived at noon. we
pulled out of the harbour an hour later. i sat at the stern. the shore
radiated with green. john saw me writing and smiled, the forest
that can be described in words is not the forest he said.

1

Several authors state that measurements taken on defective skulls indicate the need for the collection of a larger series of specimens. This was supposed to be a visceral exercise involving calculating the possibility to distinguish variation between data. Some of the samples are not large and appear similar in gross examination. I took off my clothes and became part of the forest. I am sending a small sample of my belly to my parents. Roland suggests population is necessary to account for body observations, buried in the ground, the body watching the body.

Dear Bear,

Simple forms will endure if fitted for the conditions of life. Do you believe this? We are children of the sun. If I were not labelled *mouse*, I would still be a mouse. We are what we are regardless of our percussive dimensions. Give your offspring different names and embrace the ones who choose to be lost. We all live in the branches of a great tree. Even the people listen. I can hear their insistent curiosity as they move through the forest.

Mouse

april 7  peregrination

we spent last night sleeping in the meagre cabin of the boat, anchored not far from shore. the sitka worship the sky. today we look for a suitable place to make our first camp. we approach the shore in a homemade rowboat john built. sturdy but it takes on water. the edge of the forest is just a few feet from the rocky shore. old trees collapse upon the new. we hop over the sides of the boat in knee deep water. john holds it steady in the waves while emily and i unload the gear. it takes us three trips to get everything we need off the boat. when we were finished, john rowed back to the boat alone. he told us he would be back in the morning. emily and i worked together setting up the tents.

Dear Mouse,

I can smell them. I heard them say bury their dead in the ground so you and I cannot carry their bones in different directions. It is a fragrant gift to allow oneself to let go of the world. They prefer to organize their dead, prolonging the inevitable. To them, nature is a confusion. As for you and I, they will separate the ripe flesh from our bones so they can uncover our stories from our teeth. When I am thirsty, I go to the river.

Bear

april 11   extant

we made little progress with the raft. this morning john's boat is in the inlet. there is no longer any sign of the bear. we saw a felled tree that extended like an arm out of the forest across the rocky beach and into the water. the tree is still alive. branches extended into the sky and the water. a bird perched on one branch, a starfish on another. we collected a limited number of samples. i am uneasy with the preliminary measurements. i called out to john to bring my box of books ashore. a large wave hit the side of the rowboat and the books tumbled into the water. the books floated like islands, an archipelago stretching out towards the horizon.

Dear Bear,

They reach back for me and find the howling forest with so many lines for them to follow. They are ashamed of this feat and this draws them to wild places. Now we live together, dead in their tent, the best of friends. I appreciate how careful they are with my hushed body, the procedure they follow to pull us both apart.

Mouse

april 15   fortuitist

these islands produce remarkable vegetation. this morning i
could not see the forest for the trees. emily and i found a cedar
so large, the two of us wrapped our arms around the soft moist
bark but could not join hands for its size. i am enjoying this time
with her, the words i speak to her feel so familiar in my throat.
she is not articulate when I really get down to it. i am surprised
by how many words i do not understand. everything is a bit of
a guess. we are ready to start collecting specimens. each sample
set will consist of a pair, one male and one female. we will take
preliminary measurements in the field, preserve the samples, and
bring them back to the university for detailed analysis. our target
is a minimum one male/female pair of each species.

2

The molar wings indicate that the reason for tooth length is unknown. If the molar length is known the forest can be approximated to a series of simple geometric shapes. More can be explained by swimming, as the reason these shapes dance beneath the surface of the water. Moral behavior is reconstructed via the probable history of evolution. The species within the regional circles is forced to rely heavily upon isolation during glaciation. His explanation proposed for this phenomenon is a combination of circles and squares.

Dear Mouse,

Before the scalpel she uses a thick black pen to draw lines on my skin beneath my fur. Sometimes she writes ambrosial words along the line of the incision and then reads them softly into my ear. Nature, dead in their hands becomes a story they can tell. One thing into another, we push at the edge of the world.

Bear

may 5   littoral

one new word per day, with each word the world gets a little bigger. this morning the water is the same colour as the sky. emily and i sit on the shore, catching up on our notes. we have seen no sign of john since he dropped us off. we have decided to move the camp to a nearby island. a local bear is growing territorial and giving us warning. we have such a large amount of gear and no boat. we already spent half the day trying to decide if we should make a raft large enough to move it all in one go. we agree to the necessity of the journey but cannot resolve the mechanisms of its becoming.

3

The most useful skull measurements indi-
cate adaptation to change. I see myself in
this skull collection. This is not working at
the 95% level of significance. No explanation
for this phenomena can be given, drawing
lines in the sand. Modern skulls are kept
separate from each other. I agree animals
should have pale pelage in exceedingly
moist environments. The flesh god reads the
high water mark, feeds on small birds and
interorbital animals. I got in the middle,
variation spilled out of my skull, trickled
down my chin to the soft moss at my feet.

Dear Bear,

Why does each hair know exactly how long it needs to grow?
It is natural to be curious of each other. This morning the wind
drew me to the water's edge. The whales are lost creatures, still
looking for their own island. The mind's tide, rises and falls
into the sea. Some islands are joined to others at low tide so
that passage would be feasible. In migratory birds, the degree of
isolation approaches zero. Whiskers see through the shadows
with little difficulty.

Mouse

4

A butterfly flickers in front of my face, an explanation never possible to verify. For thousands of years the problem of selective breeding materials was determined by dripping wax. It still fails to explain how each finger curls more than the last. Strong evidence suggests the injury crisis aided their resistance to the future. Hold in hand an unusual position in an attempt to alleviate pain. The other possible explanation is that isolation over thousands of years causes broken knuckles, unlike the previous hypothesis. Possible drift and selection have interacted in determining revolutionary changes.

Dear Mouse,

Our relationship with light is a function of structure. See the tree and know this. I suspect birds of many kinds are blown far by the fishy wind across the sea. In the winter I can live solely on my own fat. We adjust our sleep to the cycles of nature. When there is plenty, we eat plenty. In the winter, the fragrant world slows down, I can slow my heart to ten beats per minute. Temperature to an extent impacts overall activity.

Bear

may 11   interorbital

i am losing touch with what it means to be an evolutionary biologist. making connections must be practised daily. it doesn't happen on its own. today we arranged all specimens gathered thus far into pairs on the grass in the rain. even now these shapes are their own living things coated with the thick and heavy of the forest. the exercise yielded no significant discovery. we have committed ourselves to collecting more specimens. we agreed it is important to allow the data itself to determine further direction of the study. at this point, all reasonable conclusions will be approximations. my understanding of the forest is greater than my ability to describe it.

5

A basic dictum, time greater than mere gla-
cial isolation is needed to allow for the for-
mation of such a species. Left arm raised in
the air, face forward, forward and fingers
open. What measurements state focus on
my face. Look towards me. Conflicting skull
measurements in the sound of my voice. An
organism reflects the history of the organ-
ism itself. Your hand is broken and we can-
not rest primarily upon botanical evidence.
Even those who live under rocks and crea-
tures of flight illustrate fundamental impor-
tance. Sunlight filters down to all of us.

Dear Bear,

At the grinding dawn of life all beings are presented in their simplest form. The appearance of structure but no structure. We become differentiated by what falls on us. My eyes are learning to see in the shadows. I used to hide amongst the rocks in the silent light of the morning. Now our bodies are being presented for shipment. From life to the study of life. Biology. We rest now and become the characteristics of who we are. Only our bones are left to tell the story. We can no longer use our own voices. We have become data from which a new story will be told. A muffled theory. A new origin approximation. What is left but laying here. The story seems so obvious. I wish I could just tell them which measurements to take.

Mouse

## 6

This is difficult to explain. I am wide open looking down. I try to decide something as the ice retreats. Highly mobile animals could have recirculated from the future. The future of fish is on the beach, decomposing rag birds intact, feeding and jointly sealed. Possible interferences are moved north to the tree line as far west as the archipelago. Slice through the gills, and the mouth. You attacked to avoid the fear of awakening. Animosity is highly mobile. A fish thrusts itself into the sky and seems most admirably suited to life in refugia.

Dear Mouse,

Every forest beckons. The cedar holds us to the island. I have seen birds dive into the sea and fish jump into the sky. Lichen grows on both the tree and the stone. The sticky walls of the world are as living as we are. What will happen to us? What is the final fate of zoological specimen? Stripped down. The dust in my fur has been taken away. Your body is much smaller but has more of the tangy information they are looking for. I am more of a curiosity. We have so many similar characteristics. We breathe the same air. Our bones lay here like letters to each other.

Bear

7

The sunrise is hidden by clouds. The features mentioned are not noticeable in parts of the skull. Last night's drive to the surface reveals individual variation in the population. In a single breath, it is day everywhere. We rise, wash off the night and make our sacrifices to our veiled secrets. As usual treacherous flow between the islands and the mainland population is continuing to this day. Different individuals need variation to emphasize discriminating morphological characteristics. Each morning the sun rises.

Dear Mouse,

The kelp forest is a mysterious place. When the waves are low, sometimes I dive in for a swim. Tall trees diving down into the water. There are many strange creatures in the water forest, more than on the land. Many are older and wiser than you and I.

Bear

may 14   ventral

my understanding of this place is greater than my ability to describe it. my vocabulary betrays me. today emily found a beached whale on the shore, half buried in the sand. sun bleached skin stretched tight over white bones. the skin broken along the belly, revealing a dark cavern worn out by scavengers and decay. now home to worms, insects, and tiny winged silences. emily balanced beside the whale extending her head inside the cavern of its belly. as if bathing herself in the buoyant aroma of ancient sea flesh.

8

At the close of glaciation, otters were bare-
ly able to hold their own. Walking into the
forest is like looking into the mirror, even a
considerable distance across the open sea. I
pull the skin from my face so my flesh and
bones can hear what I am saying. Secret riv-
ers are frozen much of the year. Centipedes
crawl into my eyes and butterflies land to
take my red blood into their wings. A plastic
species finds faces everywhere in the shad-
ows. Changing habits demonstrate there
is evidence of the other existing. One spe-
cies disappears, a necessity of isolation in a
refugium.

Dear Bear,

Today she took off all her clothes and lay on the shore of the lake. Her legs pressed tight, her arms straight beside her. She started to flop up and down until she tumbled into the water. One hour later she emerged from the water singing. Droplets glistened on her smooth white skin. In a way these two are like mycelium living above the surface. They network and simplify. Though it seems as though they are still underground. A bunch of nudging mushrooms.

Mouse

## may 20   unicuspid

we are taking a day of rest. i am restless and feel compelled to go recheck measurements, but i resist. when something new arises, a potential pattern, i have to decide if it is a unique, discrete occurrence or if there is something systematic and common about it. rest is important, i am growing too close to the work. forgetfulness in moderation is critical. i must continue to forget just slightly what it is that i am doing. keep two steps behind the research, give it some breathing room. intention is a dangerous animal. today i took a long unseen arc back to where i started. i write this all back at the tent. i never write outside the tent. it feels strange to me to write under an open sky. my body is heavy, i want to step out of it and leave it behind.

## 9

The size of population in space and time like predators limit food supply. Nutrition is the result of the approaching tide, strong between the two borders. The females are apparently desperate for the related mainland species, presumably because they are better suited to the environment. A great white flash on the horizon searches this place. Once the size of instability errors are apparent the deer are now especially abundant, presumably because they support the oldest fauna. We culture our enemies, friends eat the things that hide amongst the trees. Striking characteristics lead to rapid change in gene frequencies.

may 25   endemism

remember to note the most basic characteristics and look for a pattern. taxonomy is a simple but difficult exercise. i feel surprisingly elated that the variability in the data to date is disallowing any firm conclusions. we are taking every opportunity to increase the sample size of each species. seven male/female pairs of each species. i am going to continue writing. preliminary classification of each species is decided as follows:

     a)   no tooth wear
     b)   teeth not badly worn
     c)   teeth badly worn

10

I fell asleep on this beach this morning.
Power factors facing the dispersal of the
species influence the magnitude of immi-
gration. My stomach tense I jumped out of
my muscles and noted the quantitative re-
lationship of the numerous villages within
the islands would have been frequent in the
past. No one is around but I look around to
make sure no one saw me sleeping. Testing
the effect of gene flow on nature is one factor
determining the effect of migration from lo-
cation to location. I don't want to be known
as someone who falls asleep on the beach.
It is possible that intense selection pressure
can overcome an isolated wild population.
You shouldn't be reading this. Please stop.
A delicate balance. I am running from this
work.

Dear Bear,

When I am tired, I go to sleep. When I am curious, I hold still and listen to the ear spitting questions around me. I cannot explain the tears falling like rain from my eyes. I thought they were going to eat us at first. He keeps his hands hidden inside the cuffs of this shirt. They swallow words with their eyes and ears and then vomit them out again with their wheezing mouths. In and out of their body. They share words with each other like us animals sometimes eat each other's feces. We all move things in and out of our bodies.

Mouse

june 1   condylobasal

i can hardly hold the pen today. known unknowns are a valuable currency of the research scientist. i'll leave unknown unknowns for the poets. today i found a tree exactly the same height as myself.

## 11

The straight is relatively shallow. Today I saw a muddy paw print on a tree. The print as big as my face. Radiocarbon dating from this period is indicative of the rise of the arctic ice sheets. The print the height of my face. At that time all the islands would have been connected by ice only two miles from shore to shore. I stepped to the print to smell. During some of the oscillations it would have been very useful to determine the rate of retreating ice versus the rise of sea level as a result of a worldwide melting pot. The paw print smelled like fish.

Dear Mouse,

Yesterday, despite being dead, I went outside and wrote the
delicious history of the world in ash on the rocks at low tide.
As I wrote, I forgot everything. This morning, I woke to find
it all washed away. Today, I will start over. I remember almost
everything. For a long time, I thought mice were birds that flew
along the ground. I can see now that you have no wings. I bet
you wish you could grow a pair now. I swear I saw more feathers
growing out of his back.

Bear

june 4   diaspore

this happened. i made love to a tree. we loved each other as best we could. me and the moist mossy bark. sunshine all around us. the forest is so green.

12

The four major events took years to happen. A passage across the right side of the ocean which each with a single master. Everywhere we find everywhere. The evidence of the final accounts. Two nest, two different islands. A nucleus and its wandering electrons. It is funny small restoration is considered to be forgotten with a hundred thousand years. Rise and disappear. The trees reach wide toward the water's number. The accuracy of glacial observations remark from accidental variation. An inch of water covering a strange landscape, a device to connect geological evidence to support the possible existence of refugia.

Dear Bear,

Today the woman looked to see no one was watching and stepped out of the boat into the gurgling water. When he realized she was missing he leaned over the edge. She secretly climbed onto shore on the other side of the inlet. Wherever they go they are only partially there. A part of them in the whirring past and a part of them in the future. Only their ghosts moved around in the present, looking for the parts of themselves that go back together.

Mouse

june 9   morphological

for their own protection. i am looking forward to getting journals
back to the university. i am writing to myself in the future. how are
you? i hope that when i receive this i understand what it all means.
at the moment i am struggling to put it all together. emily bounds
along the shore looking for creatures of interest in the shallow tide
pools. she is fascinated with minnows, observes patterns of their
movement with detail. she leans over her reflection, her lips slowly
open and close back together. i watch her perched in the branches
of a nearby tree.

13

Absences are interesting. Our lines curve
into their cells and become something else.
These endemic forms constitute a growing
population able to exist on other islands.
I can feel something crawling around my
heart, feeding on the crumbs. The purpose
of this paper evolved from interglacial style.
The lake is important to determine how
much contribution is made by the insularity
of the environment. These forms constitute
a growing list of species and subspecies en-
demic to the island. All animals are prison-
ers of ancestral populations.

Dear Mouse,

It is a strange hunter who does not eat their prey. Instead, they arrange them in rows and put them in boxes on their boat. Perhaps for the long winter. Sadness echoes in her eyes like thunder across the water. If like you, I could still cry, I would have wept when she looked into my eyes.

Bear

june 14   insularity

so many things in the forest do not have a name. this seems less important when i am by myself. words are more important when we want to take something with us. emily and i spent most of the day in the boat circling small islands making notes on the thickness of vegetation near the water. i broke a tent pole trying to move a rock in the tide pool. we spent an hour searching for a long straight branch.

14

Absence of evidence is everywhere. This morning I saw a fireball rise into the sky. Specimens from within and adjacent to the island increase the scope and consequence of parallel evolution. From east to west a backdrop of pink and silver. Strong evidence exists in support of these characteristics. Here in the last fascinating part of the world I am not certain how travelers maintain the possibility of reaching a conclusion. The refugia hypothesis explains revolution, evolution as a consequence of isolation. I am ready for the similarities one would expect in a refugia.

Dear Bear,

They are rhythmic hunters. Why primarily the shrew? Their hunger is academic. They fill their growling bellies with the fruit of the trees that grow between this world and the next. Already, little remains of the blue that was once the whistling sky.

Mouse

june 20   lagomorphs

so hot today we undressed by a pool in a stream deep in the forest
and bathed each other. we lay on the moss in the sunshine to dry.
fell asleep and when we awoke stood on either side of a tree reaching
our arms around to join hands and pressed our skin against the
bark, savouring the great life between us.

15

General trends among native carnivores affect the proportions of growing mice. The water has become glass, the change is likely genetic. The fat proportions of growing mice in summer temperatures leads them to the water. The general theory holds that Darwin's finches could reveal the underlying cause of this mindless paper. I saw them floating on the surface. It is possible that smaller islands have massive teeth. The disparity between the size of the sexes was emotional to say the least. The general theory holds animals have been living the same day for many years.

Dear Mouse,

Today he climbed to the top of a tall tree. He extended his eagle wings and leaped out into the air. I lost him to the sun, but I believe he actually flew. At least I did not see him crash to the ground. I wonder if you will be better at death because you are nocturnal. I loved to take sweet baths in the sunlight. They carry their own tiny stars with them at night. I wonder if I should have killed them when I had the chance. I could be rolling in the dust. Kicking it up to watch the flowery sun beams cascade into the forest around me.

Bear

june 22   quiescent

meaningful interpretation of the data relies so heavily on content. i woke to find emily missing. she returned an hour later with two cod for breakfast, soaking wet and unable to speak. i spent all day measuring the length of my worn-down teeth.

## 16

The larger size of the smaller future increases the body's descent. I do not want to put all the eggs in one basket. The pattern we bring informs the subjects we find. The names of the forest creatures differ because of their characteristics. It is not known why the rodents are small. We are preceded by our vocabulary. The sky is the most frequent general autogenetic phenomena. The problems associated with predator competitors will often be greatly reduced with the accumulation of antibodies.

Dear Bear,

Today they were on different islands. They spoke to each other across the water. They could not make each other out, could not see each other because of the fog. He spread his wings and flew across the water to find her. At the same time, she dove into the babbling water and swam across the inlet. When they each arrived, they turned and shouted back for each other. They could not understand what each other was saying. They each crossed the channel again at the same time, arriving on the other side and shouting for each other. This happened many more times. We are specimens and not corpses. We are the chosen ones because of our special features. The dimensions and wear of my clattering teeth are of considerable interest. Most mice don't live beyond twelve or so months anyway. I used to be so afraid of death and I am not anymore.

Mouse

june 28  stratigraphy

cannot work today. lower back. awake. i was done staring at the
ceiling of the tent. i hobbled to a patch of moss in the sunshine.
the grass welcomed me. sang songs to me. my stomach growled. i
stood and followed the smell of cooking fish.

## 17

There is now evidence that the local bear, weasel, and caribou have experienced genetic alteration as a consequence of selection pressure. Good books arise from similar conditions in my experience. There is no advantage to make the self a geographical priority. Further introduction of small amounts of sample size are not significant. Changes in the cell itself can be attributed to birds and mammals, killing each other over the last 10,000 years. I write what I know about morphological changes along the rim of my metal cup.

Dear Mouse,

What is the difference between the living and the dead?
Decomposition is faster than growth. Take your wounds
seriously. The living trees are the dreams of the fallen. Ghosts
are a scented echo. Sound travels in straight lines. She carriers a
dark bag on her shoulder. Today she showed me her notebook.
Leaves and flowers pressed between the pages. Colours resting
on words.

Bear

july 2   pelage

this morning the air smells of pine and yellow poplar. i have no
urge to go anywhere.

18

All forms rise as a result of insular conditions. Degree of isolation can be observed as a fracture of fossil material. The mainland conserves its species. Relics of the first history are like negotiating a climb out of a whirlpool. Looking down into the sea. Concept arises as a result of incident primata. Like tombstones, the greater range of variation has been recorded to outline the degree of isolation. Since the displacement has occurred there is an increasing body of evidence to suggest original language is a displaced relic.

Dear Bear,

The man and woman suffer from an audible madness. They need to describe the world in order to inhabit it. They are lucky they are forgetful. The sound of the world can change at any moment. Nothing softens my shrill heart more than watching the trees become covered in snow. There is nothing more terrifying than trying to scurry across a thin white layer on the ground. As soon as the eagle sees your lines, you're dead.

Mouse

july 5   ungulate

this morning i was wakened by three bald eagles in a tree above
my tent. i am surprised to find that i have grown used to her
disappearances. my throat is sore, as if i've been screeching out
through the fog, across the water.

19

The body length of most mainland popula-
tions are approximately the same size. Tooth
grinding is a source of error in small relic
populations. Living in a cold environment
at the edge of the world can be confusing.
Other factors link the isolation of dispersion
from within the group. The tree's fingers
point toward the sky. Tall stacks of spiders
are difficult to place. The remains of other
factors know that sometimes it is impossible
to point at anything other than the sky.

Dear Mouse,

Great sickness, great flood, great famine, great war, great fire, great boredom. Thrive and multiply. Something is always coming. Those best adapted to sudden change are best positioned for survival. The refugia story has some merit. The aromatic world will tell it again and again. We do not choose this. Seek an island you like the smell of, if only for a little while so that you may differentiate yourself from your brothers and sisters. They make maps with their bodies. Trace landscapes on pieces of paper, tear pieces out and start again.

Bear

july 9   ermine

i spent the last three days immersed in hot pools. i followed a trickle
of tepid water up the rocks through the moonlight. i lay down at
its source. i awoke at sunrise to feel the hairs on my chest growing
down into the cracks in the rock.

20

I found a crab on the beach today. The larg-
est species occur on the most distant islands
claws and legs torn away from the body.
Other explanation considers islands sepa-
rated by a few miles. I could feel its muscles
living inside its shell. Microclimate could be
a correlation between the degree of isolation
and bite size. I toss the crab body into the
ocean and watch it disappear towards the
bottom. It is difficult to obtain complete
measurements for each population.

Dear Mouse,

Great sickness, great flood, great famine, great war, great fire, great boredom. Thrive and multiply, this the prime directive. Something is always coming. Those best adapted to sudden change are best positioned for survival. The refugia story has some merit. The great flood story is an old one. The world will tell it again and again. We do not choose this.

Bear

july 12  concomitant

this wind is both mandolin and clarinet. i have not bothered to
leave the tent, there is no chance of crossing the inlet today. the
waves are right outside the door. i catch the drips in a pot and
drink it when it gets full.

july 15   pleistonerene

on the verge of afternoon sleep i saw a line of light on my shoulder.
a strand of hair glistening in the sun. i draped it over a tree branch
and watched it dance.

21

An outline of literature statements insert characteristics of different mammals. The final selection of mushrooms on the grass at the edge of the meadow. The fact that not all large mice have proportionally shorter tails due to the forms on the mainland is now established. A patch of flowers and a tail in the long grass. I reached down my hand snapped I felt its back break between my fingers. I have assumed that the changing size of the ocean includes lagomorphs. I dangled it in front of his face. He puts down his magnifying glass and swallowed it hole.

Dear Bear,

Today he inserts tail feathers, painstakingly pressing each feather into the base of his spine. Blood ran down his leg, he spread his wings and soared out over the water. He extended his screaming talons down into the water and pulled out a fish. I listened with every bone in my roaring body.

Mouse

july 19   occam's razor

the words inside the books began to make unrecognizable noises
and it was then i realized i was dreaming. a wild man came to the
door of my tent. his hands were filthy as if he had been digging
deep into the earth. i warned him that the books were hungry and
by their sounds, ready to attack. i wonder now what simple thing
he might have asked for: food, a blanket? all day i kept my eyes out
for footprints in the sand.

## 22

Islands prove useful and show the greatest increase in body size, eggs are laid in the new ground. Mainland head/tail ratio is less than one. I can hear them chirping in my ear. There used to be a tendency to become smaller and smaller. Qualitative information is significant to the 95% level. The potential sources of forms, the birds flying every which way. I am afraid to walk over the grass, I walk through the shallow water instead.

Dear Mouse,

A beached whale is a feast for all of us. Some of us eat it from the outside in, others from the inside out. We meet in the savoury middle and laugh. Sometimes we eat each other, some accidentally, sometimes on purpose. Once we are bones, the fire will comfort us. It is our outer flesh that feels like pain. Once the fur and skin has burned away from our bones and become like hot rocks. This is the shape that will truly tell our story, not these antiseptic screams we make as we are dying.

Bear

july 21   ascribe

together everything smells sweet like the earth. we spent the morning paddling to the small islands in the bay to check trap sites. emily cut her hand today walking up the shore from the boat. we try to become human because it is necessary. an axe in one hand a notebook in the other. she tripped and fell on the axe. i was terrified that the bleeding would not stop. we are at the edge of the world.

july 26  taxonomist

emily and i spent the morning circling each other and arranging
specimens into near identical pairs. outside it rained. water flooded
the earthen floor. emily kept reaching down to splash water on her
skin. her back glistens, her belly is so white.

23

We danced on the beach this morning. This section has outlined some abundant opportunities for error. The mice living on these islands are close relatives of all basic forms. The published descriptions of measurements taken by different collections are lines in the sand. The mainland forms in one population compare with the basic island morphological trends. with a pair of scissors cut circles with no reference to how big or small. Without stating the size of the sample, it is impossible to compare subspecies.

Dear Bear,

They are hunters of language. Have you seen them with their clicking pens, making marks in their notebooks? Come winter they will eat their words. Crunch them like fish bone fragments, stick to the corners of their mouths. Why are they so afraid of the forest burning? The tree of life will survive as its branches extend beyond the limits of the sky. Let go and float into the amber fire.

Mouse

july 29   soma

clearest night since i've been to the islands. a raven glides almost unseen across the sky. fisherman waved us down as we crossed the channel. a storm blew him far out to sea. he sought refuge in the archipelago. he offered us 16 crab which we accepted with delight. we boiled the crab in a pot of water. we picked at the delicious white flesh and flicked bits of shell into the fire as the fisherman told stories of the dark shadows of submarines and looming towers of ice.

## 24

Samples collected within the second hypothesis have been modified to be anti-invasive. Rain so heavy on the tarp it sounds like typewriter keys. A story starts to form in my mind and the wind blows it all away. Radio taxonomy is summarized diagrammatically. I am comfortable in my understanding of the story even if I cannot find the most important assumptions in this hypothesis. There are many complicated explanations that can be explained by the forest. It is unlikely that evolutionary history will be apparent according to commonly proposed theories based on fossil evidence. What kind of story do you tell to the forest?

Dear Mouse,

The water is rising, this intoxicating rain will not stop. I listen to them talking about moving to higher ground. This island has so little high ground. Who knows when this will cease? The man and the woman are loading animals onto their boat. Today she slowly stroked my fur for hours. She was hesitant at first as if I might wake up and sink my teeth into her fruity arm. We both know I am not asleep.

Bear

july 30   strata

we are at the edge of the world measuring the skulls of mice. the islands are slowly inhaled and exhaled by the sea. i am concerned that my limited understanding of geography will prevent my development of a useful relationship between the biological and stratigraphical evidence for refugia.

august 2   scintilla

today i watched emily swim. the sunlight shimmered on her almost recognizable belly as she glided deep beneath the water. i counted to four hundred on one submersion. she returned to the surface gasping, surrounded by a school of fish.

25

A solitary tree stands at the edge of the water at the edge of the forest, leaning out into the wind. The complete absence of fossil evidence negates the retreat of the glaciers. The story of animals told by specimens from within and adjacent to museums to increase the scope of the islands the consequence of parallel evolution. Animals tell stories through people as well. The strongest evidence in support of these characteristics lies in the fascinating area of future work. The black dots on the graph, tooth wear vs skull size, skull size vs maxillary row, maxillary row vs tail length, tail length vs degree of isolation.

Dear Bear,

Today the waves were thunderous. So much sea foam around the rocks. The woman was naked, rubbing sea foam over her body. Washing the land from her skin. She rubbed so hard her nose and ears gradually washed off. All of her hair as well. The skin between her legs fused together and a sharp fin grew from the centre of her back. She is kind. I can tell by the way she broke my neck. Pressure in just the right place. A quick click. She made it easy on both of us. My body intact, the data unobstructed. I've watched him throw others into a pail of water he keeps outside the door of his tent.

Mouse

august 4 littoral

this morning the waves rose as we tried to cross the bay. the current rushed out from the inlet and swept us out to sea. what worked against us hardened our intent. we paddled hard toward land. it took days to reach the shore. we stepped onto the beach, cold and exhausted and felt the soft gravity of the trees welcome us home. for hours afterwards, emily gazed longingly at the waves lapping in the bay.

## 26

In the intervening fifty years one major change has occurred on the islands, rats have been introduced. A sandpiper stands in the water. The birds are watching me today. On islands without rats this theory would have to be explained with a range of body/ tail ratios. I listen to their chatter as I write this down. The ecology of the species on the island is necessary to understand particular examples. An accurate assessment of the evolution of the denominator, larger and more agile. Beaks poke at the grass near the shore, looking for creatures hidden away from the light.

Dear Mouse,

Today the human male gathered eagle feathers from the forest floor in the fragrant pines near the shore. One by one he plunged them into the flesh of his arms. He stood on the beach with his hands in the air as blood trickled down his body to the sand. I can feel the fish in my rancid belly begin to bubble and bloat. The other creatures inside us are starting to take over. All along they await this great and final feast. Last night I could hear you laughing in your sleep.

Bear

august 7  maxillary

while walking through the trees along the shore i saw emily on the rock staring stonily at the water. she professed her love for biology as the tide rose around her. the clouds opened and sunlight shone down in a yellow beam onto the water.

27

The relic theory is complicated due to the great number of islands and species. The door to his tent was open. This is the result of recent distinctive character proportions, specifically body/cranium ratio. This island is small with a high population level. He is sick in bed, sheet pulled up to his chin. Tent smells like wet feathers. The distribution of forms uses evidence against the relic hypothesis. He muttered in a different language. Island creatures arise from a common ancestor. His head seems to float on the pillow. He asked me for a glass of water. His lips trembled, blood ran down his chin.

Dear Mouse,

The kelp forest is an odorous place. When the waves are low, sometimes I dive in for a swim. Tall trees diving down into the water. There are many strange creatures in the water forest. More than on land, I think. Many are older and wiser than you and I. I was worried this would happen. The light is fading. I can feel myself slipping somehow away. The light is like dawn at sunrise but grows dimmer. The opposite of what one would expect. My ability to describe it is diminishing. Soon there will be nothing left but my stinking body and the bullet still bouncing around inside my brain.

Bear

august 10   peregrination

today i removed my clothes and lay down on the forest floor. the damp moss cradled my back and sunlight poured down through the leaves. i fell asleep and dreamt i swam in a river of blood. i awoke to find emily writing in the margins of her book.

28

It is possible small mice were distributed
across the islands by geese. A seal sleeps on
the beach. A more plausible explanation is
some islands have had multiple introduc-
tions. Body extended, chin rests on his chest,
black eyes closed. Characteristics of isolat-
ed and semi-isolated populations thrive on
the post glacial shoreline. I want to go lay
down beside the seal. The apparent break-
down is the size of the population living on
the island. Wet skin drying in the sun. The
theory of common origin has become sus-
pect, when considering the explanation of
rapid evolution. I lay down and feel myself
remembering.

Dear Mouse,

Termites and mushrooms do slow and important work. Without them the land would be a great pile of sticks and bones. They prefer the shade and the darkness. The light they use is old light, held deep within the flesh of the trees. They sit and watch sunsets from hundreds of years ago.

Bear

august 12   eustatic

this morning i woke before sunrise my chest tight. my arms trembled, could not focus on the work. i walked into the forest a long ways. found a shallow hole in the ground and knelt within it. i beat the earth with my fists. i screeched until my throat was sore. blood and dirt stained my knuckles. i sank my fingers into the soil and listened to the circumambience of the forest.

29

Distinctions between recently collected specimens indicates that perhaps the populations are genetically less stable than previously believed. We are exhausted. The electrophoretic patterns suggest the species are conspecific. We lay down and stare up into the blue sky through the tops of the trees. We laughed and then we laughed at our laughter until the laughter sounded like laughter laughing. The analysis of body/tail ratio used in different measuring techniques is adapted for the present study. Figures are available for all specimens.

Dear Bear,

Mussels cling to rocks for their entire life. Like a tree they take rest and remain in one place while the rest of the world moves around them. I am restless, movement is my shell. When something frightens us, we can dart to the left or the right to escape. In the end it doesn't really matter. We feel rumbling terror when we just sit still. Variation arises from mistake much more so than crashing intention. This is what creates the different colours in the flowers.

Mouse

august 20   depauperate

this morning i forgot how to eat. i pressed my lips to the bark of a tree. this island has provided an exciting number of samples. i am surprised at how skilled i have become at gathering specimens. i spot them from considerable distance and then swoop down with my fingers. last night i dreamt i was sleeping on this island and when i awoke i was on the same island. i don't know what i am trying to say. there is nothing in my head and i am trying to write it down.

30

Observations reveal belly stripes are never present when breast spots are absent. I lay on my side looking at the green rising out of the forest floor. Eleven of twenty-three samples have elevated pigment. I swear I hear singing. One skull is asymmetrical. I feel my lips and realize it is I who am singing. No words, just notes. The suggested introduction is a place for more variable size. The colour of the grass swaying back and forth.

Dear Bear,

Is it you that has been eating the broken moon? Each night another piece of it is missing. Soon the night will be in complete darkness. The darker the night the louder the sounds become. The owl can find us even if it cannot see. I would ask that you please stop eating the moon. In the spring when the trickling water carries death from the land the creek can turn golden as the plants dissolve and allow themselves to be carried to the sea. It is as if the water itself is filled with brassy sunlight.

Mouse

august 29

today we found a large net washed up upon the rocks. emily looked pale and silent as we unhooked it from the rocks and rolled it neatly, placing it beside a log along the shore. i imagined the net itself, a creature floating in the sea, passively catching its prey, looking for a new land, a place to call home.

31

The main consideration is not significant to 95% of the outliers. The samples from the archipelago have both real differences and those attributed to age. Visitors do not return from some islands. Group differences reflect the point outlined in the previous sentence. I am cautious to look to the first points joined by a line. The formula for this calculation will be listed in appendix 1. I look down to see all the flesh from my bones has dissolved. The main consideration is whether the results appear to be meaningful. I pick up handfuls of mud from the ground and fill in my arms and legs.

Dear Mouse,

The killer whale is no more killer than the rest of us. No better
hunter. A killer whale has never caught a mouse. Once a killer
whale tried to catch a bear. It came out of the sea. The bear gave
chase and led it deep into the forest until it was lost. The animals
of the forest surrounded the whale and laughed as it wept but
then we felt bad, so we ate it and returned its bones to the sea.
The floral light is changing for me as well though I can still feel
the wind as strong as ever. I can feel it rustle through my fur.
I can feel these words crawl into my body. I imagine myself
floating on my back on a vast body of water.

Bear

september 3

last night i dreamt i was deep in the forest and could hear a telephone ringing. i followed the sound through the shadows until i came to the carcass of a mule deer. the ringing emerged from its rotting skull. i leaned in and whispered, hello. the ringing stopped there was a pause of silence and then a click. the dear carcass leaped to its feet and sprung into the forest. all day i have been thinking of a way to reestablish the connection and return the call.

32

The most important statistical analysis is caused by wide age spread. This rock is a good place to sit and watch the ocean. Some skulls with defective measurements are plotted against sample variance with no observable correlation. Everything was silent until I realized I was on fire. Logarithmic transformation not accurately measured by the clouds. If everything in the world is asleep the restrictions are used to test homogeneity. How much power in these lines, the maximum value of any element. I feel frustrated, restless, and ineffective. This function index indicates a high degree of isolation. My mind spills out onto the beach and chases a rabbit into the forest.

Dear Mouse,

The gulls are squawking loudly today. They fly this way and that, searching for stench. When their feathers fall, they float on the sea. They know something is about to happen. Today she had a feather tucked behind her ear. It as though she found it in the water. The dark fibers clung to each other.

Bear

september 15

today we inventoried all of the samples we have collected and doubled checked all preliminary measurements. so many dots that need connecting. some many numbers penciled into tables. i measured the teeth of a mouse and then quickly ate it, tearing its flesh from its body with my teeth. it was too late, i realized emily was watching. when our eyes met she simply shrugged and returned to tabling numbers in her notebook.

33

Looking at the taxomonical characteristics employed in the city are associated with the greatest amount of pigmentation. The rest of what pattern emerges demonstrates present techniques within the realm of variability within the species. Everything always goes back, mistaking one thing for another. Time counts from the point of application. The differences between populations can be detected with protein electrophoresis and hemoglobin electrophoresis. Nothing left but a familiar taste on the tongue.

september 18

i am going to miss this place and am not longing for the conclusion of the journey. i already sense this will be a place to return to. a beehive in a pine near the beach is humming. there is no wind today and the water is clear and calm. in the distance the humpbacks breach and crash back down into the water. i extend my wings and fly out to see them.

34

In future discussions the body line will be unimportant. It is hard to decide how to lay on these rocks. The body has enough secrets to become a trap. I found it on the edge, toes resting in the water. The other message shows considerable variation. waves roll back and forth over my foot. Sexual variation in genes tends to observe variation between populations. I have become a fish out of water. This rock knows me by how I found it. Variation within the wild population. I fall asleep and when I awake a starfish is resting on my belly button. The sun has set and the moon is in the centre of the sky.

Dear Bear,

I have tried many times to run on the surface of the water. I am not fast or slow enough. I always fall through. Have you tried this? If I keep trying, I may someday get it. My chest feels empty. My heart has left my lifting body and wondered back into the forest. I know it cannot see nor smell but somehow knows where it is going. Someday I hope it can write so that I know who it is doing.

Mouse

september 28   dorsal

the shape of the growing data is still too open. i am reluctant to
make any decisions. early this morning i watched two deer swim
through the forest. last night i dreamt i peeled a piece of lichen
from a tree and ate it. on my way to john's boat, moments before
the tide came in i noticed a message drawn in the sand as if by
the moon to the sun: watch how much i love you, see how much
i suffer. john brought me a box of books from town to replace the
ones lost from the rowboat. i sat and read on the shore for a while.
john watched me while pretending to scrub algae from the hull.

## 35

The discussion will proceed with the analysis of characteristics of our ancestors. I lay down on my side and make an imaginary camera with my fingers. Water plays a critical role in development. I snapped imaginary photographs. There appears to be no relationship between the samples of change. I take another and another. Pressure plays a part in developing the unifying pattern. Nonflammable factors have been discussed. Infinite sunlight reflects off my chest. I take one last photograph, shake out my hands and the camera disappears.

Dear Mouse,

All life comes from and returns to the sea. Today he cut away
the sour flesh on his fingers, so his hands looked like talons.
The eagle feathers, red and sticky with dry blood like an eaglet
emerging from its shell. I can hear a coppery ringing inside my
head. I suppose what I need to get done is done. How long do we
love on after our hearts stop beating?

Bear

october 4   dentition

these islands isolated in space and time provide a tangible dataset from which conclusions can be drawn. i know it. i see signs of a pattern, a partial story, the pieces of the puzzle are fluid and change periodically. today i saw a black bear sleeping in a shallow hole beside a large rock. its body expanded as it breathed. it scratched its belly with its long claws. rolled onto its belly and walked to the shore. it reared up on hind legs and held its paws out in front, as if for balance. i am growing less afraid of the bear. power arises out of the imbalance of need. at this point, the bear and i have little need for each other. i did not tell emily about seeing the bear today. there is no sign of john or his boat. he should arrive any day now.

36

Age is the most important indicator of age.
I lay back on the forest floor. The skull study
relies on tooth wear diagnosis. A deer skull,
old from the wear in the teeth. Pregnant fe-
males have been excluded. The eyes are dark
and silent. The age structure of different pop-
ulations is rather subjective. Unfortunately
many questions for tomorrow. Consequently
I want my belly to look whole. Change in the
eyes takes place gradually, another size mea-
surement must be used.

Dear Mouse,

This is the end. It is not that I have nothing left to say but now would rather keep my musty words to myself inside me to keep me company. You are the best of friends and I sincerely appreciate sharing this leg of the journey with you. I will always be your friend and we will always have these letters between us.

Bear

## 37

The relic theory has been advanced to explain facts that necessitate a new explanation. Trees believe in silence. Science is a powerful and general effort. I lay down beneath the canopy, this is necessary to attempt to explain. Only older skulls could be saved and occasionally only the measurements. I am a crystal when I sit down to interview specimens. Specimens were collected at every opportunity until finally forced into extinction. Only the skull can describe language. Everyone talking in a roar. It will be necessary to attempt to discuss which environment will require analysis.

october 10   extant

when i speak to her i feel as though words are the worst way to
transmit a clear message. there is this thing and then the next thing.
a sense of the other, tugging. tonight by the fire, john called out to
the sky. she moved her arms as she spoke, shadows danced on the
trees behind her. not everything in the dataset can be understood
by the data itself. a blink and things shift, one thing into the next.

38

Circumstantial evidence indicates we are recognizably different in at least one characteristic and therefore do not obviously belong to one ancestral population. The main difficulty with this accounting is the fact that you are not rapidly subject to change. I can feel myself smiling, explanation has some merit. I started talking but did not understand what I was saying. Large collections from many islands do not obviously belong to one ancestor. The relationship of the different characteristics is unknown. A conclusion limiting the number of islands from hypothetical diffusion could fill any gaps in the present study.

Dear Bear,

I spent my life looking for seeds in the shadows. I want to sputter and choke but have been dead for too long now. Your letters have meant the world to me. I wish I could take them to whenever it is that we are going. Perhaps I will go back to the beginning and reread them as I finally fall asleep.

Mouse

## 40

Animals raised in the laboratory eat different food on the beach. Inhabiting mice can significantly alter the most general skull parts. Populations primarily indicate that animals are older that previously suspected. Some rodents wear teeth down at different rates. The fog allows us to look at the sun. Even animals in the laboratory are influenced by a more sebaceous state. The counter parts are glowing on the horizon, a hundred feet away. I haven't the slightest idea what I am saying. I write this way so you'll have a hard time pinning me down.

october 20   palantine

it took us four hours to unload all the specimens off the boat and package them for shipping back to the university. john made coffee on the small stove in the galley. we explained why we need to extend the expedition. we have decided to stay, i am not sure for how long. emily and i are not the same as when we arrived. we stood on the shore and watched the boat embark for the mainland. sea gulls flew from the rails and soared for the trees along the shore.

## Acknowledgements

Leanna Baxter for your enduring love and support. Burke, Liam, and Alice, my energy and inspiration. Nora and Norval Horner. A special thanks to Lee Yee Gamble for your continued encouragement and wisdom throughout this project. Lisa Rose Berreth-Feragen. Leslie Greentree. Selina Clary. The 2004 Sage Hill Poetry Colloquium: Steven Ross Smith, Gerry Shikatani, Louise Halfe, Breckan Hancock. Sharon Drummond, Kari McCrea, Kamal Parmar, Ruth Pierson, Norma Rowen. The Copenhagen Writers: Sara Rahmeh, Marianne Hansen, Nina Holm-Jensen, Bjarke Alexander Larsen, Evangelos Mylonas, Marilag Dimatulac, Aldo Ricardo Aleida Robles, Subramaniam Ramasubramanian, Dennis DuBois. Write Club: Lee Yee Gamble, Elana Krol, Doug Horner, Henry Campbell. The Single Onion: Kirk Miles, Paul Marshall, David Martin, Laurie Anne Fuhr, Lori D. Roadhouse. The Drunken Poets Society. The Happiest Hour of All: Micah Stone and Andre Rodriques. Jeremy Hill my old friend and traveling companion who remains on an island to this very day. Helen Hajnoczky, Alison Cobra, Melina Cusano, and the University of Calgary Press.

This book was inspired by a trip taken to Haida Gwaii, islands of the Haida people, an archipelago located off the northern Pacific coast of Canada.

Photo credit: Francis A Willey

PATRICK HORNER is a Canadian poet and engineer living in Copenhagen, Denmark, where he works to develop new water treatment technology. He co-wrote and co-produced *Waste Dump*, a serial radio play, and his poetry and fiction have been published in *Wax, Dandelion, Broken Pencil,* and more. *Refugia* is his first book of poetry.

**BRAVE & BRILLIANT SERIES**

SERIES EDITOR:
Aritha van Herk, Professor, English, University of Calgary
ISSN 2371-7238 (PRINT) ISSN 2371-7246 (ONLINE)

Brave & Brilliant encompasses fiction, poetry, and everything in between and beyond. Bold and lively, each with its own strong and unique voice, Brave & Brilliant books entertain and engage readers with fresh and energetic approaches to storytelling and verse.